Castles, Caves, and Honeycombs

LINDA ASHMAN

Illustrated by LAUREN STRINGER

Harcourt, Inc.

San Diego   New York   London

Special thanks to my editor, Allyn Johnston,
who knows when to gently push me back into shape
—L. S.

Library of Congress Cataloging-in-Publication Data
Ashman, Linda.
Castles, caves, and honeycombs/written by Linda Ashman; illustrated by Lauren Stringer.
p. cm.
Summary: Describes some of the unique places where animals build their homes,
such as in a heap of twigs, in a cave, or in the hollow space inside a tree.
[1. Dwellings—Fiction. 2. Home—Fiction. 3. Animals—Fiction. 4. Stories in rhyme.]
I. Stringer, Lauren, ill. II. Title.
PZ8.3.A775Cas   2001
[E]—dc21   99-50801
ISBN 0-15-202211-2

First edition
H G F E D C B A
Printed in Hong Kong

The illustrations in this book were painted in
Lascaux acrylics on Fabriano 140 lb. watercolor paper.
The display type was set in Gasteur.
The text type was set in Throhand Ink.
Printed by South China Printing Company, Ltd., Hong Kong
This book was printed on totally chlorine-free Nymolla Matte Art paper.
Production supervision by Sandra Grebenar and Ginger Boyer
Designed by Lydia D'moch and Lauren Stringer

Many places make a home —
A heap of twigs.

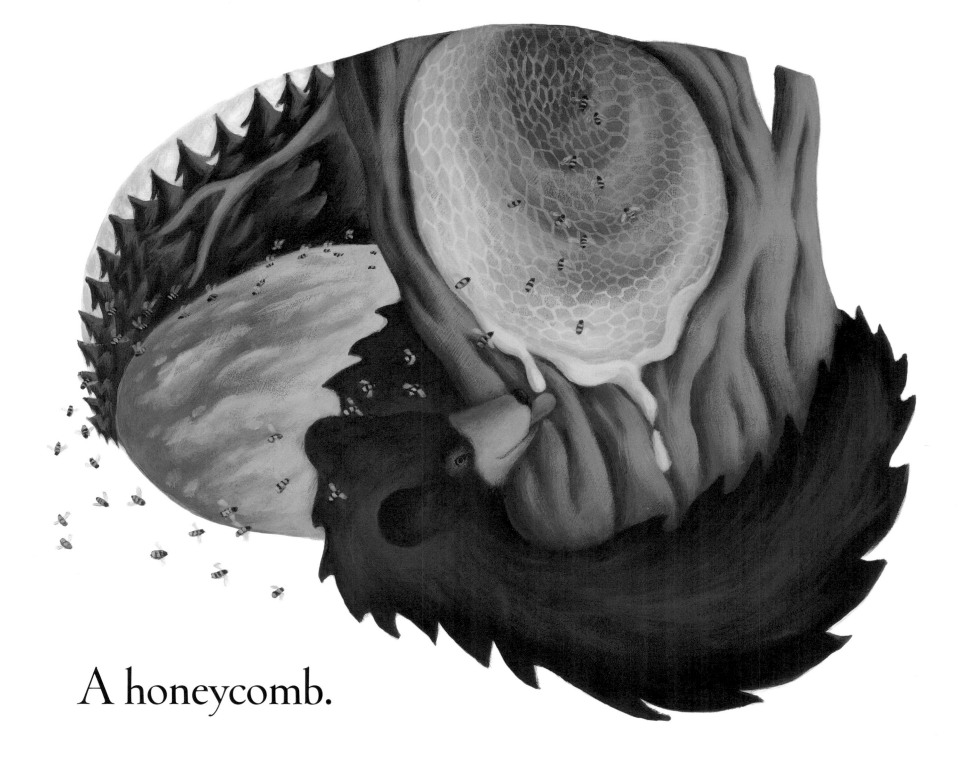

A honeycomb.

A castle with
a tower or two.

An aerie with
a bird's-eye view.

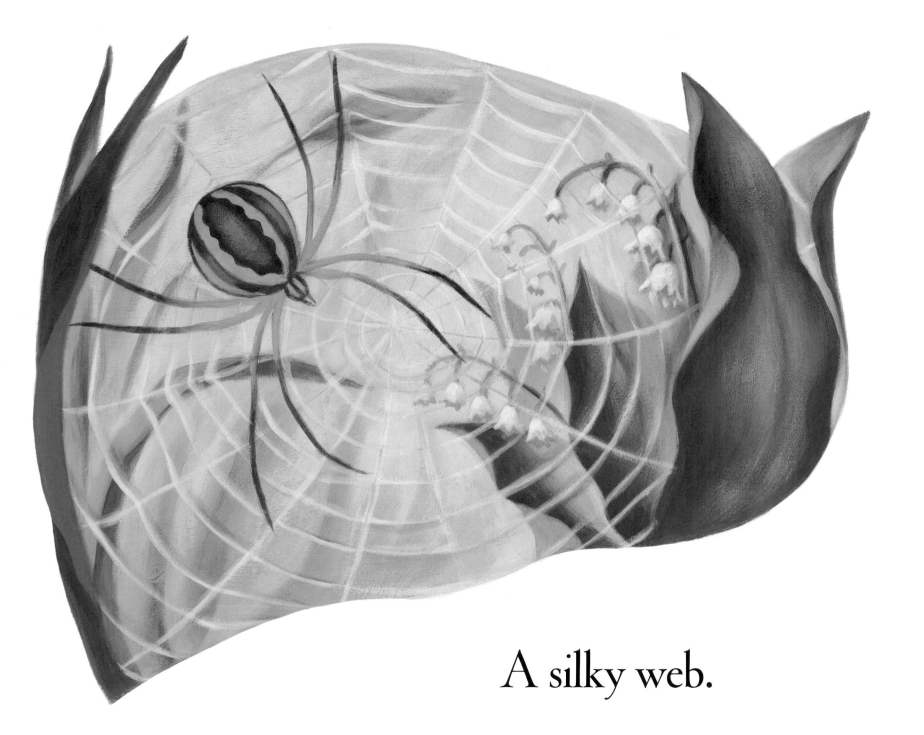

A silky web.

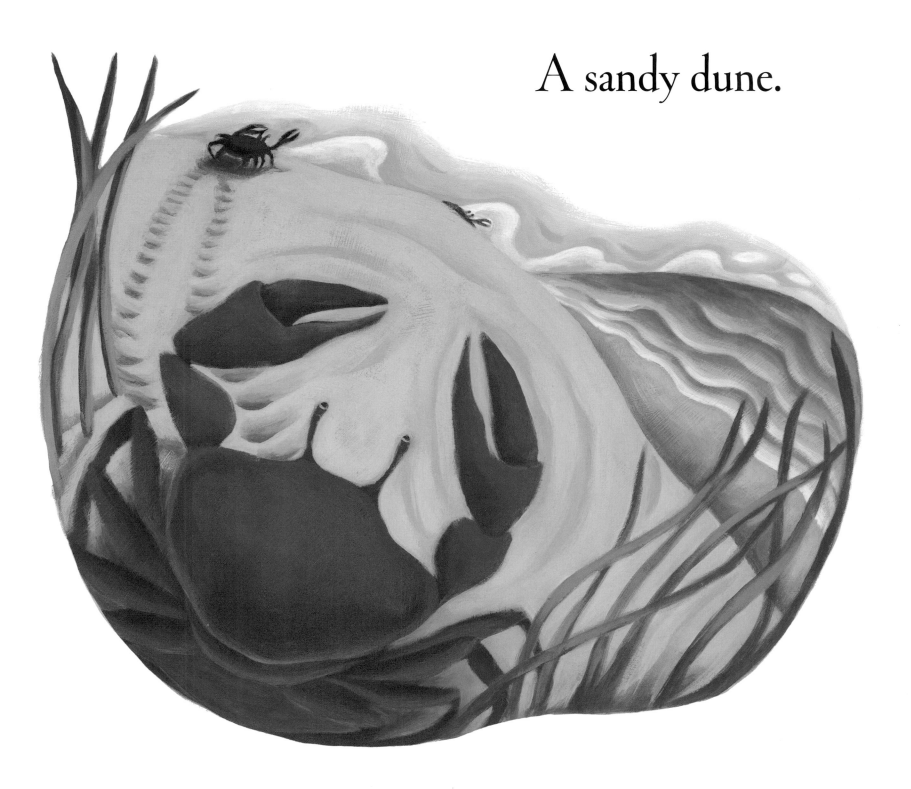

A sandy dune.

A room inside
a warm cocoon.

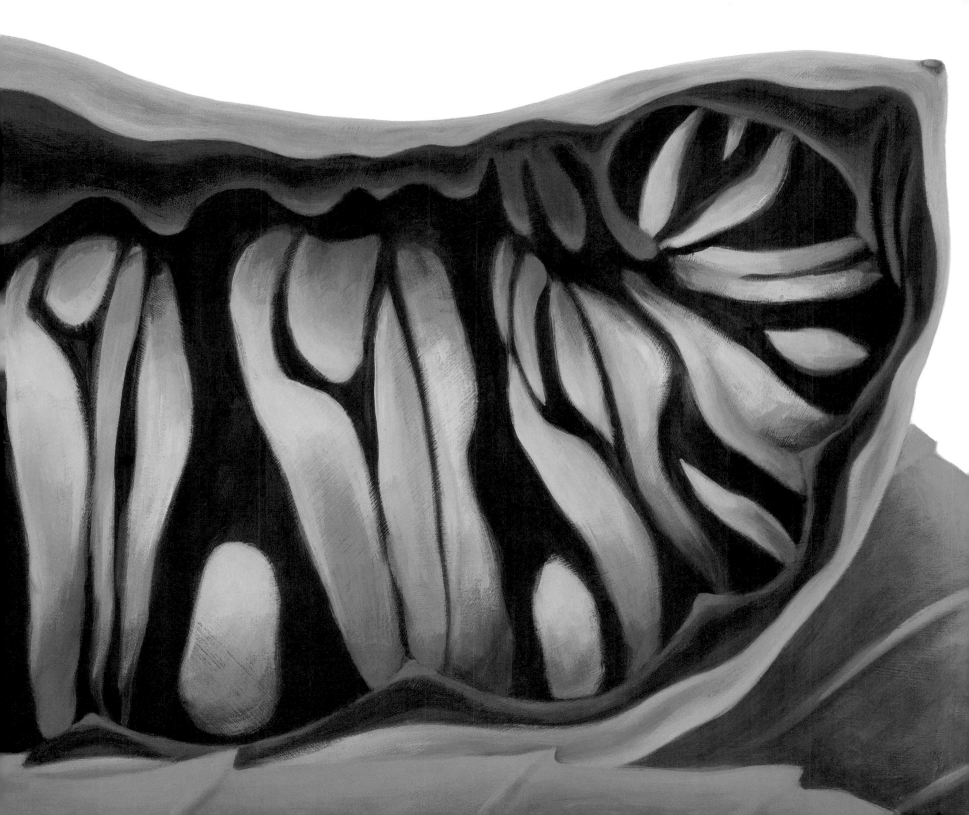

A chamber in
a snowy mound.

A busy town beneath
the ground.

A silent cave.

A secret den.

A warren in a grassy glen.

A sloping cliff
above the shore.

A hole beneath
the kitchen floor.

A rocky pit.

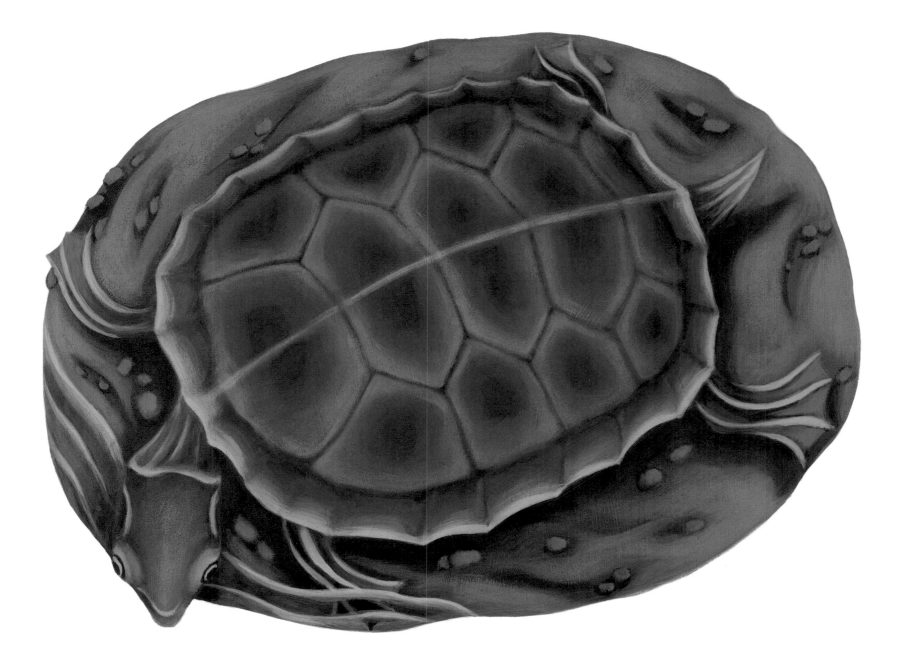

An armor case.

A shell that's carried place to place.

A hollow space
inside a tree.

A tidal pool beside
the sea.

A home's a house, a den, a nest.

A place to play,

A place to rest.

A place to share,

A place to hug.

A home is someplace
safe and snug.